BOOK OF WATER

BOOK OF WATER

Andreas Philippopoulos-Mihalopoulos
Translated by Sakis Kyratzis

ERIS

57 Berkeley Square
London W1J 6ER

eris.press

MIX
Paper | Supporting
responsible forestry
FSC® C013604

Contents

the lake is the others

Doorstep

The first thing he did when he woke up was to look around him. The walls of his room were rocking. The large roses– the central feature of a wallpaper he never chose–were floating against their beige foliage. He held his breath. If he didn't move, if he didn't stir the air, maybe then the roses would calm down. He exhaled as softly as he could, and the room finally settled. Now he could breathe again. He got up and opened the door. Everything was swaying. He knew this trick wouldn't work for the rest of the house, but he thought he'd try just in case. They had left him some tea and biscuits on the kitchen counter, which he started eating slowly, careful not to drop any crumbs. The kitchen faced east, and the light was usually bright yellow. The cupboards had already started lulling up and down the way they usually do in the early evening, when dinner is prepared. The only thing missing was the clunking of the cutlery as they got ready to sit at the table. He held his breath again, but he quickly gave up. He placed his cup in the dishwasher and opened the kitchen door. The water had risen noticeably during the night and the waves were crashing against the doorstep. Nothing too ominous. Soft round waves lapping against the doorstep. He took off his pyjamas and stepped into the water as quietly as he could. The light was almost horizontal. The surface was flat, polished metal, and on it wavelets, light and honey soft, teetering sideways and around, just as he imagined waves in a fjord would. He sunk his head in the water and looked around. There was a gurgle of activity: seaweed, fish, pebbles reflecting light and then disappearing, dunes moving along the seabed mirroring the waves above. Green and gold. He let the first bubble go and waited a little. After the second one, the water started to forget him. When he finally let go of all the air inside him, the whole watery mass with its grainy sandy base and all the seaweed, fish and pebbles had stopped moving. Everything expanded like a wave of time, gigantically slow. They had forgotten him somewhere amidst their folds, they let him observe the pause. He was content: this time, it took less than usual. ◉

The Wave

I don't know how he does it, but he's always eating into my space: a little here and a little there, always whenever I'm not looking, in the middle of the night when we finally succumb to our yielding knees and rest, or in the morning when I'm looking for something to eat. He pushes the partition I've made, supposedly by accident. He even coughs to cover the splash, but of course I know what's going on. I'm standing there as usual, with my back against the partition, knees slightly bent, and bang! he jolts and throws me off balance. And with every new push, he inches further into my space. The moment I realise, I yell and push back. But it gets tiring. I run out of patience and give up. Let him have as much space as he wants. What is he going to do with it anyway? As long as he doesn't leave me with nowhere to stand, I'm happy with what I have. In any case, when the big one comes, all this will end. Like this woman who's gathering wood every day or sometimes metal sheets of some sort, God knows where she finds them; she even brought in a whole door the other day. She has put together something that resembles a shack or a phone booth and she shuts herself in there. She's added some plastic climbers hanging from the ceiling. Why plastic, I ask her, it's not as if we don't have enough water to water them. I haven't got the time nor the will, she says. In any case, everything is temporary. It's true. No one's safe, it's a jungle out there. Fights everywhere, bickering over whose is what. Only one thing can save us all, the big one, when it comes. If it ever comes. My grandmother used to tell me what her grandmother used to tell her, about how she was standing in the water when, years ago, the big one came. It didn't just come from the horizon as you would expect. It came from everywhere at once: a howling rain so dense you couldn't see your hand, waters rising with rage, as if the earth had opened her breast, finally ready to let out the cry that would destroy everything; and at the same time, the horizon turned black and a mile-high wall of water started approaching, slowly like a promise, the waterfall of ages starting from the feet of an idle god and charging straight to all those below waiting with open arms and knees bent from desire. Some mornings, especially when the sun is late to rise, a whisper stirs the water surface, words dart past us whistling that some-thing enormous has appeared on the horizon, a boulder of water perhaps, so dense that it seems opaque and fi-nal. But until now, nothing has arrived but clouds, heav-enly taunts casting their shadows on us. And we, neither human nor beast, remain stranded in the shallows of the lake covering the globe, a lifetime of waiting, tepid and uncreased water barely rising to our knees, each one of us stubbornly confined to our allocated little square of water, drowning in the melancholy of the desire for one more inch of space. ◉

Book of Water

He reopened the book after five or ten minutes. The story was not bad, though not very well told. He had nothing else to do, so he went back to it. He knew he could carry on reading for another fifteen, twenty minutes max. The cover had already started to soften and suck his fingers in, like an aquarium floating in the atmosphere of his hands. When the book eventually turned a greenish hue, he knew he had no more than a minute left. He tried to read faster but, anxious as he was, he found it impossible to understand what he was reading. He was forced to reread the same parts, hoping he would understand them the second or third time. Before the minute was up, just at the moment when he knew he would have to give up the book, the same thing always happened. He could never tell whether he liked it or not. The book would start liquifying, its pages turning into undercurrents and its phrases into reflections of geological lassitude. And yet it did not seem to dissolve like any volume of liquid would, nor would it slip out of his hands. It remained there, somewhat sticky but also teasingly present; like green apple jelly mixed with brown sand, dulling its lustre. He liked that phrase and, if he could, he would hold it in his hands for longer. The problem, however, was that his fingers–perhaps his entire hand, up to his arm and further up, maybe eventually his whole body, including the room with all the furniture and the window with the afternoon light streaming from outside and the city with its sounds and the world with all its squeaks–it seemed to turn into liquid, more liquid than

the book itself, an encompassing sparse density, light like
the wind, slow like the sun, hazy like an ending. He finally
let the book go, not because it was slipping from his hands,
but because he himself was slipping from the book, like
a character no longer demanded by the plot, dragging
down with him a piece of the world that was held together by liquid bridges, stretched ropes made of jelly, trembling hands of waves. Maybe what bothered him was that,
in fact, he liked this watery fall. More than anything, he
liked the hush he could just hear the second before letting
the book slip off his hands and the world return to water. ◉

At Lela's

She would often invite me over. I went with pleasure. She was one of the few–perhaps the only one–I was not afraid to visit. With the others I felt a numbness, almost a shiver, the moment they invited me, a malaise, a hint of fever that would suggest itself before I even considered the trouble of visiting. But at hers it was different. Everything seemed to fit, to have its place–even the smells had their own little boxes–and I was allowed to open all the boxes, drawers, cupboards, play with the ornaments or rummage through the kitchen shelves. She would smile and encourage me while we talked about politics, twentieth-century classical music, cave paintings and quantum physics. I'm sure there were corners she did not want me to touch, but perhaps, as she smiled and talked to me about various things without any hesitation or embarrassment, she guided me discreetly away from those corners and towards others she did not mind my exploring. I was never really aware of this. I always felt safe, at ease, better even than at home. We would usually go through the various rooms together, her swimming next to me at a steady pace; I, more curious, often stopping to dive below, searching for something interesting that might have previously escaped me. We would rest on some shelves–my favourite ones? or perhaps hers?–and let the books open at random and the paragraphs float on our palms. Chance was important. Only then did time stop, or at least slow down, become amniotic fluid and feed us the future. We allowed for chance things to occur, like biscuits whose flavour changed from packet

to packet, from bite to bite. When the music stopped, usually opera–was it her that stopped it without my realising
it?–right in the middle of the track, a flawless dive like a
metal blade slicing through the soprano's breath, at those
points time lagged, pooling in shimmering valleys as if
by a waterfall for us to bathe in. I still believe, even now
that I'm writing this, or at least I want to believe, that nothing was guided, everything was left to chance and time
slowed down for both of us, equally. ◎

The City

She always began with the streets. She drew them on the ground with a twig–not necessarily parallel, or even straight. She just let the twig lead her. Sometimes she covered the whole area close to the slides. She filled it up with streets, alleyways and byways, tunnels, boulevards five or sometimes six lanes wide. Then she made room for the water, either a river cutting the city in half, or canals intersecting the streets, or a bay stretched beside the city. In any case, she always made bridges bringing together the various boroughs arching proudly over the ditches, which she then filled with water from the playground's tap. She left the buildings for last. Her city didn't have a centre and outskirts. It was all mixed together. Sometimes the noisy district with the tall buildings and the museums rose where the shadow of the plane tree fell; other times, she placed it a a bit further, near the see-saws. In between them she would always scatter little houses for the elderly, the refugees who had just arrived to the city, children who wanted to live on their own surrounded by animals, and other friends of hers. Once, she had the mayor live in one of these small houses. Why not, she thought. But most of the time she placed him near the City Hall–a large building that always required many cartons–next to the cathedral. She wasn't particularly interested in making her city pretty. In fact, it usually resembled a rubbish heap ready to be recycled. People who saw her wondered, how can this child play in such filth? Her concern however was something different: her city never lasted long enough. It's not that other children would come and ruin it. No, they all knew she was odd and avoided her. The problem was her. More than the streets and their baroque curves, more than the walls of the museums and the shops, more even than the roofs and their antennae, what she liked the most were the windows. As soon as the walls were up and the rooms started to warm up and become more habitable, she went about tearing the buildings apart in order to open up windows, big or small, narrow or gaping wide, left open so that the sun-drenched water could rush in. And the outside would flood the inside with watery embraces, wide chambers of frothy waves swallowing up the buildings. She never managed to complete the city. Sometimes she would begin a new city right there, in the middle of the previous one, when the buildings had already turned into mud as the water engulfed them and the bridges had collapsed, as if they were made of rum-dipped sugar cubes. All her cities suffered the same fate. And in the end, she would climb on a piece of carton and float out in the open, pushed by the aquatic boulevards and the submerged palaces that gushed through the windows. Maybe that was her city after all: an oceanic metropolis of failed beginnings. ◉

Open Sea

He sets out in the boat every afternoon. Just him and a bottle of water. He's never frightened, even when the sea is rough. He goes steady, as if following a line on the surface of the sea visible only to him. At times, winds and currents rush him on; at others they delay him. Still, it always takes him exactly the same time to reach the end of this line. Observing him from the shore, one would wonder how, despite never hurrying or delaying, he always seems to glide over the weather and arrive where he is supposed to arrive at exactly the same moment. But no one sees him. The line ends somewhere in the middle of the sea. Not an island or a coast nearby. Nothing to get your bearings by. But as soon as he arrives, he pulls the paddles in and grabs the bottle of water that rocks back and forth on the bottom of the boat. A simple, plastic bottle, one and a half litres, no label. There may have been a label once, but now not even a trace of glue. Without getting up, he holds the bottle with one hand and unscrews the cap with the other. He starts pouring the water into the sea. As soon as it's empty, he sits up slightly, and, holding onto the edge of the boat, sinks the bottle into the sea and lets it fill with water. Once filled, he screws the cap back on and returns following the same invisible line. He leaves the boat on the shore and walks a few feet to the house. He enters the room where the other one is sitting. He doesn't seem to be expecting him or realise that someone is entering the room. His armchair stands in something like a small children's pool, one of those inflatable ones. The pool is empty.

He sits there patiently, without moving, as the water from the bottle flows slowly over his head, through his hair and onto the bridge of his nose, his half-closed eyelids, his shoulders and his chest, forming a shallow reservoir between his thighs, then onto his feet, ending up in the inflatable children's pool. The water appears to fall slowly, as if it gained viscosity on its way from the open sea. It lingers on his body for longer than anyone would imagine, dallying on his recesses and mounts, deliberating before diving off the tip of his jaw onto the top of his chest. It helps that the other one is not pouring it in a hurry, no hurry at all. Quite the contrary. He is very deliberate, stopping the pouring, checking, carrying on with just a trickle, stopping again. As though he's expecting to see some movement, some reaction, a trembling. At times something happens, like the quiver of the basil plant when watered on a hot summer afternoon. But before the afternoon is over, he'll have gathered all the water from the pool, put it back in the bottle, and set out with the boat again. ◉

The Shepherdess

He barely ate. Not even sweets like the other kids. Everyone begged him to eat something, even his classmates at kindergarten. He ate so little, it was a miracle he survived. He only drank water. He began with the feeding bottle, and as he grew older he learnt to drink from a glass. He outgrew the glass and started drinking straight from the fridge bottle; when he eventually outgrew even that, he started gulping it with his hands as he caught it from the tap. And in the end, even without his hands: he stuck his mouth to the tap and drank, not wasting a drop. His parents tried various methods to convince him to eat some food–even that rather despairingly unpedagogical idea of serving him the same meal for lunch and dinner so that he finally gets used to it. After three such days of failed attempts, his mother entered his room and asked him what he wished to eat. She would cook for him whatever he wished. Sat calmly in his small yellow armchair, he said, I'm just a little thirsty. One afternoon, his mother took him along to visit a friend of the family. Her house looked like a museum, immaculately appointed, expensive ornaments and porcelain everywhere, delicate biscuits and glossy chocolates he could never touch. His mother and her friend were chatting away in the kitchen. They had left him in the living room sipping his water from a crystal glass. Oh he is a good boy, never one to cause any trouble, oh yes, he is always well-mannered and on his best behaviour, yes thank you, I know we have done a good job, never up to any mischief, such a sweet boy–just this one blasted thing, his eating habits, if only he would eat a little more so we wouldn't have to worry about him at all, but what can you do, he barely eats anything, we have tried everything, we can't help it. As soon as they heard him groan, they ran into the living room. He had picked up a porcelain figurine and had crammed it in his mouth, so deep it got stuck. His mother was in such a panic that she could not stop screaming. Keeping her cool, her friend cautiously managed to remove it. The figurine was of a shepherdess herding her three white sheep. Her dress was glossy grey. In one hand she was holding a brown cane and in the other a bucket. The bucket was half full, a porcelain surface that rose up to the middle, white and bright like milk. It could almost have been milk. Or water and they might have just neglected to paint it blue. The first thing he told them when his mouth was free was, I do not like shepherdesses. ◉

the blue is here and
it's not going away

Tornadoes

Sometimes she'd let the washing pile up in the sink for days. Making a start had always been her problem. Once she finally got round to doing it, she'd forget herself. The kitchen window, like all the windows of the house, looked out onto the sea. As she was doing the washing up, brush in hand, scraping off the remains of busy days and of numerous snacks, sweat dripping from her forehead into the slurry of the stack, the water outside appeared to rise and become one with the water inside, like a tidal sink. There were never any bathers in the sea. They preferred the western side where there rarely was any wind. On this side of the island, there was nothing else but wind-often blowing the windows open and rushing in like a tornado scouring everything up in its wake. Sometimes she even imagined that the Ajax tornado, or whichever cleaning brand it was that had that ad, with the muscles and the loop earrings, came in through the kitchen window and feverishly cleaned, not just the dishes but the entire kitchen. She often saw such tornadoes reach her home from the sea. It wasn't a genie though like the tornado in the ad. These ones were men, women and even children. Their muscles were wasted, their earrings long sold and their eyes red after hours, maybe days, of fighting with the sea. She took them in and gave them whatever food she had. How do you think the plates stacked up! She didn't eat much anyway-just a quick bite, always in a hurry, hardly ever using a plate. Sometimes she found scraps of their boats. She'd pile these in a corner of the garden.

You never know when they might come in handy. She had
kept everything ever since that day when she lifted the
whole house along with the garden, the shed, even the
broken swing that had been hanging for years from the
fig tree, and threw it all in the water, with the woman and
house becoming an island rooted in the open sea where
the streams of two continents and centuries of fear meet,
the whole thing a solitary beacon devoured by the waves
day and night. Ever since that day, she treasured whatever
washed up on the edges of her garden, because you never
know. ◉

Garden

"Copenhagen Cherry Tomatoes? What's that now?" She had no idea you could grow tomatoes in Denmark. Perhaps in a greenhouse, but then you wouldn't give these tomatoes a name! "Could they be those dried ones, you know, those green and unripe ones? And anyway, why on earth would they like this sort over there?" They would have to wait to find out: the tomatoes were still in seed. Patience, perseverance, and so on. But she couldn't deny her this. They had moved to this house on the edge of the city only because it had a garden. The garden was small and round the back of the house. But in the midday sun, the blue walls held a promise, even though right now they only held soil and weeds. She thought the left-hand corner would be just right: vegetables, then herbs, flowers at the front, and–space allowing–a narrow patch of lawn. For now, they only had the cherry tomatoes. "You'll have to water them every day though. Tomatoes need a lot of water, even Danish ones I guess." She needn't remind her. Every morning and every afternoon, when that corner of the garden was left in the shade, she picked up the watering can she'd bought especially for the tomatoes and kept on a nail on the wall on the left as you came through the garden door. She filled it with water from the kitchen (they did not have enough money yet to do up the garden and put a water tap there) and watered the whole area until it was soaking wet. In spite of their efforts, weeks passed and not even a sprout had pierced the soil. "Do they need more water?" she wondered. So she made it a habit to water them with every glass of water she drank. A glass for her, a watering can for the tomatoes. Gradually, and while still nothing green was peeking out of the soil, water began to cover the surface of the garden. The garden was clearly not deep enough and could not absorb all that water, so it began to well. At first, it was only a few inches deep, and she could still walk there and carry on her usual watering without too much difficulty. But as the days passed, the level rose. It was Saturday morning when they realised they had to swim up to the left corner of the garden where the seeds slept tucked away. It wasn't that difficult: two strokes and you were there. The garden was that small. She'd hang the watering can on her shoulder like a bag and swim there to water the area afresh. In the evenings, they sat with their backs to the TV, facing the glazed garden doors that looked like an aquarium. The whole lounge swayed along the reflections from the street lamp outside. The soil seemed fixed at the bottom, just like coffee dregs, and over it danced strips of light, silky, evening streamers from the party next door. When the weather got warmer, especially in the midday sun, they'd put on their swimsuits and float on the surface of their garden. Towards the end of July, half-asleep, lulled by the watery caresses, something tickled their backs. From deep in the waterbed, in the middle of the garden, cherry tomatoes, round, bright red, were bubbling up like a fountain and bursting against their backs. ◉

Coffee

It was happening more and more often, though he still could not predict when. He made the coffee in exactly the same way: in the same pot, the same quantities, the same fake alabaster cup, the same tray just big enough for the cup, the same glass of sparkling water and finally the same small piece of chocolate. He always sat at the same place on the balcony-he wouldn't fit anywhere else anyway-always the same time, same view, everything the same, as much as possible of course. But it remained unpredictable. Since he put so much effort into making it happen, one would think that he had a burning desire to relive it, every day if possible. But he did not even know whether he really wanted to. He always ended up so upset and breathless, it could not have been good for him. Nevertheless, he felt a stiff impatience, especially lately that the odds of it happening again seemed for some reason to be growing. Yesterday, for example, it had happened before he'd even finished his coffee, when the dregs were dazed by the remaining liquid over them, and he could still distinguish his forehead reflected on the glossy surface. Just as he was lifting the cup to take the last sip, the cup opened and narrowed at the same time, leaving him holding the entire globe in his hand like a well, deep, narrow and dark. His hand was heavy, and his whole body tensed to keep him upright. The balcony tore away from beneath him, his feet plunged to the ground, his head burnt by the sun. He turned into an elongated globe, a dappled column of water, rushing but contained, a well flooding without overflowing, never, not a drop. His body was trembling under the weight of this molten economy, his hands sliding over the column that might have been his own body, a colossal sphere or an earthly spear, he could not make out which. And in this suspended flight, as skies and oceans swirled in the cup, the water shattered abruptly, the column dissolved in a waterfall, his hands were burned by the overwhelming sun, and the earth rose like a huge bubonic wave to become a balcony rushing beneath his feet and finally give him a place from which to see the world. But today, nothing happened. He finished his coffee and made a mental note to water the geraniums in the evening. ◉

The Collector

He was a tenacious hoarder. He told himself he was a collector, but that was probably just to cover up his obsession. He knew he wasn't really a collector. He had no intention of completing his collection, he wasn't searching for specific pieces, he didn't admire his collection, he didn't flaunt it. As much as he'd like to call himself a collector, something inside him was saying 'delector'. It wasn't a very successful term, but it came to him one day by accident, thinking it could signify exactly the opposite of collector. Mornings like today excited him no end. Still in his bed, he could hear nothing. Absolute stillness, bar some soft wavelets plopping on the beach. Barely awake, he rushed out. If he had not been mistaken, if the day was indeed without even the tiniest breeze, with all the waves still asleep and the sea as flat as a stagnant lake, a uniform flatness extending between sand and water, he would stop dead in his tracks and try to calm down. The main thing was his breath: it shouldn't come out abruptly and cause any agitation. When he felt he could control it, he turned sideways and slipped into the water. He was always careful not to make any waves: his movements were geological, his breath a universe of morning slumber, even his gaze emptied out and dissolved on the surface of the sea. When, after years of slow moving, the water finally reached the middle of his chest, he got to work. He cut pieces out of water and a bit of sand, like dessert slices with pastry at the bottom and clear jelly on top. Perfect square pieces, gently quivering just as he detached them from the sea

and let them float away. He wasn't worried, they wouldn't
go far, the sea was calm. Gradually he surrounded his
perfectly still body with a number of water pieces, an iridescent fleet pulsating all around him. He didn't stop until
the sea changed, which it did. Even the lightest wave would
wake his body from its ancient lethargy. He picked up the
pieces and slowly came ashore. He carefully took them
home and immediately stored them away. It wasn't easy
anymore. Drawers were full, cupboards were brimming,
bags and suitcases were stuffed. He had already started to
take out the bedroom floorboards and cram in the pieces
wherever he could. Sometimes they suffocated him, they
were that many. He would go out to the balcony to breathe,
but even there he would find himself surrounded by more
pieces–who knows when he put them there. Even the pots,
the hose and the drain hadn't escaped this fate. No peace
for him there either. His greatest nightmare however was
this: what if the pieces started to spread like saliva, vis-
cous jellyfish crushed by the planetary movement of centuries of hoarding, and started dripping on the heads of
his downstairs neighbours or flooding the footsteps of the
upstairs tenants. He would then have to show the pieces
to everyone, talk about them, explain why he did it. He
would perhaps have to confess that he was a delector. The
times the nightmare ended well, this was usually enough,
and they understood what he meant. But when it didn't, all
the words would leave him, and he could not speak of the
pieces. ◉

Volumes

His mother never had to worry about his swimming too far out. He was always scared of the deep. The few times when he felt that his feet were hovering over deep waters, he got so anxious that he had difficulty breathing. He didn't know why but a phrase always came to his mind: volumes of water. One day, it suddenly occurred to him that the word 'volume' referred both to mass and books. Since then, the water under his feet had been replaced by a tall, labyrinthine library, filled with endless shelves of heavy volumes. At times he tried to step onto the top shelf, where the bookcase ended and no more books were kept, but he was always just a few inches short. The odd thing was that he wasn't really afraid of the deep when his head was below the surface and his eyes were open and looking out across that blue maze. His fear then transformed into something else. Awe, maybe desire. He did not know exactly what he desired, but he seemed to want to swallow all that volume of water, and at the same time to be swallowed by it. But as soon as he came up, head popping up on the surface, he would begin once again to splash about fitfully, breathing shallow and intermittent breaths. He never managed to stay below the surface for long. Except that one time, when he almost felt the upper shelf with the tip of his right foot. It was as if the sea-shelf had spread enough to let him perch. Surprised, he looked down, his head submerged and his eyes open, and saw all the volumes of water arranged neatly next to each other, colourful but also translucent. He could almost brush

them with the tip of his foot. It seemed to him that some
of the volumes were half-open, grinning mouths ready to
swallow him, not threatening this time, but gentle, like a
breeze coming down a hill drowned in honeysuckle. But
the moment he tried to place his foot on them, the mouths
shut. Perhaps he had not yet swallowed enough of their
wet paragraphs. ◉

Holidays

We should start closer to Christmas, she said. Just before, says the other. Better to start just before, so we won't get anxious about Christmas expenses. It arrived every week, usually on Thursdays. She had to fetch it up from the post office because the postman wouldn't deliver it. She left work a little early, stopped by the post office, gave the notice to the employee (was it always the same one? were they different? she couldn't tell) and waited. She knew she would have to hurry home as soon as she got it, so while the employee was looking for it, she would ready herself to spring into action: bag on shoulder, cardigan buttoned up in case she got cold, keys within reach. As she watched the employee carefully approach the counter, her hands would join in a large but impermeable embrace in which the employee would place the water. A quick thank you and off home. Not so hasty that it spills over, not so slow that it slips through her fingers: she was proud never to have wasted a single drop. At home, her bag barely dropped from her shoulder, she would rush straight to the piggy bank and slowly tip her hands, a waterslide between her stretched fingers and the narrow slit on the top of the piggy bank. The water would swish in, and whatever little leaked out she would gather with her fingers and push it in. With all of the water carefully saved, she would place the piggy bank back on the top shelf of the bookcase. It would sit there patiently until the following Thursday morning, when she would have to remember to take it off the shelf before leaving for work.

She'd had it for ages, couldn't even remember from where. It was a useless thing sitting in the cupboard, until they started saving and she dug it out. It gave her great pleasure to watch it gradually get fuller and fuller, expanding from within and taking up more and more space. It even changed colour with each deposit, or it might have been because the top shelf was in direct sunlight all day. In any case, the original pink had begun to fade, turning week by week into a sky blue. By June, the blue had turned deeper and darker. It was even iridescent, especially in the evenings, when the smell of the terrace jasmine made her feel lightheaded. By mid-June, she could no longer put it back on the shelf–it had grown too heavy. She left it right there on the carpet, in the middle of the living room. As the early July heat intensified, the piggy bank bloated so much that it covered the whole carpet. She moved the television to the bedroom–there was nowhere left to stand in the living room, let alone to sit and watch her series. At the beginning of August–it was a Tuesday morning–a sea breath spread in the living room, and the whole floor filled with water. Gentle waves pushed against the walls, dissolving them, making them giggle and gurgle. Salty water covered the terraces of the whole neighbourhood, and the children began to swim from veranda to veranda. August had become an endless liquid horizon perched on the upper floors of the buildings, a garland of waterlilies stretched from aerial to aerial. Holidays. ◉

Geometry

He had developed an obsessive habit of going for a swim, rain or shine, at exactly three o'clock every afternoon. In time, he had to limit this only to Sundays. But he never missed a Sunday swim in his life. His swimming style had always been gauche, evidently self-taught and serving a purpose rather than made to look good. Nothing compared to the beautiful mechanics of other swimmers, heads elegantly following the arch of their arm, heeding a call from within their own body, sliding over the waves as if truly belonging. His was all noisy and fractured, making it up as he went along, arms diving awkwardly, violently breaking the water, his head bobbing in and out as if detached from the rest of the body. Perhaps because he never learned how to breathe when swimming and was gulping water instead. His inbreath was filled with waves, his outbreath mixed with overworked drool. But there was one thing he always did almost methodically: he only sucked in the water when his head was turned left, always on the side of the heart. And he exhaled the water a couple of arm lengths later, but always to his right, head still dipped in the water, web-like saliva flow entering the body of the sea. Despite all his shortcomings, he was fast and could carry on for long distances. He had once seen himself swimming from above (a documentary on winter swimmers or something, they wanted to interview him but he did not feel like it, how to explain that he wasn't really a swimmer, let alone a winter swimmer really). He was ashamed of his swimming style, he was afraid they would

say that he could never be a real swimmer, thrashing like
this as if he were a poodle. But he agreed to be filmed
from above, just as a background to the voiceover. They
even had a helicopter–oddly big budget for something as
insignificant as that, he thought. Months later, they sent
him the video. He did not manage to watch the whole
thing–he got bored and, anyway, it was not so much about
winter swimmers after all. It was about people swimming
in polluted waters, desperate people risking lives in various places around the world. He knew the sea was polluted of course. He did not realise it was so newsworthy, and
he hardly changed his habits even after watching this.
On the contrary, after watching himself from above, his
body became even more determined, as if steeled with a
mission. He had seen something when he watched himself
from above that he could not have known otherwise: his
body was moving along a line so straight and precise, cutting the waters so perfectly, that at first he really doubted
it was him swimming. But it was him, he recognised his
trunks and his awkward swimming style. It was as if the
line was there before him and he was simply tracing it
with his body, allowing it to emerge from underneath the
water surface. But no, he was the one making it. He could
see that clearly. It was a windless day when they filmed
him, the sea calm, looking even calmer from high up. Yet
the sea was split into two. The water on the left of his body
was soft and smooth, lulling wavelets licking the air, a
lake-like constancy unperturbed by his awkward flaying.

39   And to his other side, the water was rippling with a strobe striation, filled with flashes of incandescent reflection like a pool busy with kids at lunchtime. From high up, the whole sea surface was split into two, smooth and striated linked up by that perfectly straight line he was tracing on the water. And right in the thick of this line, at its very birth point, his own inconsistent arm movements and his head splashing in the waters, mouth open swishing and spitting, mixing waters while keeping them separate. ◉

underwater passage,
seabed membrane

Underbelly

So what? Does it really matter that there are no streets? We can swim after all. Look, there are much more serious problems to occupy ourselves with. For instance, yesterday when I had to pop to the supermarket to buy something for lunch, I forgot to bring a waterproof bag and I had to go back because I didn't want to buy another one. I already have too many. Or when we find ourselves on dry land and they haven't got towels and heaters at the ready because they're not used to us, and all they do is make fun. It's great though on holidays, when they come from all over the world to marvel at us. During Easter, for instance, it's very busy but also fun, especially when we're leaving the church with our lit candles, in the hope that someone might actually manage to bring the holy light home intact. This might appear to be simple, but we have to co-ordinate with other family members, friends etc., to agree on who will be swimming in formation below and who will stand on the shoulders of others, balancing with their legs apart and arms akimbo, just like the Colossus of Rhodes holding the torch, so that they keep dry from the waist up and bring the flame home. We snub boats. We only use them to transfer large things. And even then, others come from out there with their boats and their language and their weird yells, and they transfer for us the things we need. It costs a lot, but it's worth every penny. I think we scorn boats because if we use them, then this thing might never happen. Not that it happens all the time. But when it does, especially when we swim at night and the light from the windows is reflected on the canals, that's when we are all glad not to be using boats. So, as we're doing our usual strokes and we're thinking whatever everyone thinks when they're coming home from work or going out in the evening, we sometimes decide to give in to this thing that's pulled us into the deep ever since we were born and maybe even before: a collective rumbling in our underbellies, like seaweed hands pulling us under, further below the gold green surface, deeper still than the dark green almost brown of the seabed. On that level something else begins, like a city, which we sometimes call the foundation and at other times we don't give it a name, and we talk about it through bubbles that come out of our mouths when we meet down there. And as we go deeper and deeper, our eyes pour out and become one with the steaming water at the centre of the earth, our hair tangles with other hair from other bodies and weaves a mythology of womb, and our feet float on air from other planets. We become one with everything down there, with friends who happen to be in the deep at the same time, with tourists who got lost and accidentally ended up there, with the dead and the ones that might never be born. But also with winged and glassy bodies, with trembling stamens and slumberous roots, with the whole city above and even higher, with a universe that ceaselessly swims in a borderless water bubble. ◉

Membrane

She never really believed that the bottom of the sea was dark. OK, sunlight couldn't reach all the way down those breathless vertical miles, but she had heard about all those tiny fish, molluscs, plants, and even plankton that were luminous and phosphorescent. She had no idea whether the light emanated from them or whether it was simply a reflection of something else. But she was not interested in exploring the matter further. Even if she knew the answer, it wouldn't be of much use to her. What she had to focus on now was staying hunched, avoiding straightening up her body at all costs. She really could not afford to do this. The two times she let it happen, she'd felt she was in great danger. Her head had touched, almost slipped through, a membrane so thin and brittle that it could crack at any moment. Fortunately, it didn't. But it was hard not raising her head. Not only because her back was hurting from all that bending, but mostly because it was only by raising her head that she could finally see the other side of the membrane: a gigantic drop of ocean, succulent and luminescent like an emerald eye, held together by an eyelid breath so thin, so elusive, a glaucous membrane of aether pulsing beneath the weight of aeons of water, struggling to keep the water from escaping. If the water did escape, it would surely flood the narrow tunnel beneath the bottom of the sea in which she had been gingerly burrowing, safely bent all this time. At least the tunnel was not dark. The light from the bottom of the sea splintered into waves, making her pulsate to their rhythm. Sometimes she thought that this tunnel beneath the seabed did not just reflect the light but was bearing the weight of the whole ocean above. That without this air tunnel, the bottom would swallow the ocean with everything in it, living or not. Whilst she was careful not to break the membrane with any sudden moves, she also felt the need to keep her shoulders constantly glued to it. No doubt: she held the membrane in place. She might even have been carrying the whole thing on her shoulders. She wasn't sure but she certainly felt responsible. The few times she managed to drift into some half-standing half-slouching sleep state, she dreamt that the light of the ocean finally switched off. She could then rest on the floor of the tunnel beneath the bottom of the sea, wrapping the membrane around her like a light blanket. ◉

Twice

His grandmother would always get confused and call him by his father's name. My child's child is twice my child, she would say. It reminded him of Russian dolls, waiting inside, ready to appear through the horizontal slit of the larger doll. They had a number of these brought to them by a colleague of his father's from the Ukraine. They were modern ones, however, figures of international politicians instead of Russian matryoshkas. He once picked up a couple, a large Brezhnev and a much smaller Bush, and secretly took them to the beach. He made sure that no one could see him. He jumped into the sea and tried to fill Brezhnev with water, with Bush ensconced inside. But it wasn't easy, because Bush would pop out as soon as he tried to shut Brezhnev. Eventually he succeeded. Brezhnev, much heavier now that he was filled with water, found his place back on the shelf with Bush of course hiding inside him. He re-ordered the dolls to cover the empty space left on the shelf. No one noticed. The following nights he would get up and check on Brezhnev, just in case he had started to leak or had somehow cracked open. He liked the stillness coming from inside, even when he shook the doll vigorously. He'd managed to fill the interior of the doll so perfectly with water that Bush never touched the walls. Nothing to betray his whereabouts. The whole thing was, of course, heavier–but perhaps not by much, since Bush was hollow, a balloon filled with air, floating in water. After a while, the whole affair was forgotten. It suddenly came back to him many years later, while he was sitting lotus position at

the bottom of a pool, having released all the air from his
lungs and watching, enclosed by the emerald walls of the
pool, the water surrounding him. He wondered what had
happened–perhaps Brezhnev's inner walls had bloated,
leaving Bush wedged between them. Or perhaps Brezhnev's bottom had eroded, and Bush had slipped out like
a baby between moist thighs. He had no idea what had
happened to that doll collection. Meanwhile, he began
to feel the need for air. But he liked it down there. So, he
searched and located the last molecule of oxygen within
him: twisting his waist with that characteristic creak, he
let out of the slit a smaller self who slowly rose up towards
the surface. He took him into his hands, opened him gently
and sucked the air locked inside. ◉

The Bottle

He felt thirsty. That dry mouth feeling he often had early in the morning. He hesitated. The bottle was next to him, and all he had to do was stretch, grasp it, sit up and open his mouth. Even thinking about it was exhausting. Maybe he wasn't thirsty after all. A dream came to his mouth, like the taste of last night's dinner. It was about a glass of shimmering water: clear, crystal water but very tranquil, flat, still, dead. If he drank it, a venomous calm would spread inside and freeze him. Was this sensation part of the dream or did it come to him now that he was thinking about it, he was not sure. He turned to face the wall, green wallpaper, autumn lawn colour, slightly soiled. He was inside the bottle. In the dream, he was sure he was swimming inside the bottle, perhaps even trying to hang from the edge, to get out. And then what? Would he let himself slide down on the surface like a drop of moisture? He took a deep breath, surprised that he did not feel more anxious and distressed after such a dream. He started getting up, slowly, begrudgingly, careful not to knock the bottle over. He put his feet down and stopped. He bent down, lifted the bottle with his hand, brought it over his head and turned it over. The water flowed on his hair, down his shoulders, all the way to his feet. It flowed as if the bottle was bottomless. Around him, the room began to fill, slowly at first and then rapidly, a sweltering tide pushing the surfaces and covering his desk, the picture frames on the walls, even the top shelves of the bookcase. The bottle slid out of his hands and rose up to the surface. With two large,

calm strokes, he joined it up there. He held onto the edge
and looked at the day ahead. Only a couple of clouds in
the sky, nothing to worry about, he would ride his bike to
work, and if it rained, he would just get a bit wet. ◉

Down There

The first time she rented on her own, she got a studio flat on the second floor of the building where her parents used to live. Although not really her style, she went for bright colours, soft furnishings and curtains. At the time, it seemed right. She spent some relatively happy months there until she heard that the penthouse had become available. She moved immediately, soft furnishings, curtains and all, but she no longer liked them. She turned minimalist, white surfaces and little furniture, to give free rein to the incoming light. She considered herself very fortunate to have found this flat: the water had just begun to rise and within a few months it had already reached the second floor. Everything became harder. The doors were blocked and needed extra effort to keep them opening and closing. The plants on the lower balconies had started sprouting seaweed on their stems and shells on their petals. When taking the lift, people had to hold their breath until the lift reached the second floor. In the office block opposite hers, they had installed special underwater motors to keep the lift going, since all over the city the lifts had acquired the habit of detaching themselves and floating on the surface like air bubbles. She felt especially house-proud when her friends visited and marvelled at how dry everything was and how magnificent the city looked through the windows, half-sunk in the silver horizon of the world's laguna reflecting the afternoon sun. But she gradually found herself going down to her old flat on the second floor and spending more and more time with the lady who now lived there. They did not have much to say, but she liked it when she was served hot barley coffee in those floating cups. The second floors were by now on a level with the lapping waves, their surface glistening like cream on top of hot milk. The whole flat was sliced across the middle: below the surface of the water lay carpets, TV sets, and coffee tables, their stillness refracted on the flat's seabed; above the surface, high chairs, paintings and standard lamps were mirrored on the water like reeds surrounding a still pond. What she most enjoyed was sitting in the arm-chair, her back straight and her head upright, the water reaching halfway up her face. Her eyes then opened and deepened, taking on that dark blue shade only found in the open sea, while before her, coffee cups floated on the porcelain of the afternoon. ◉

The Skeins

They always begin after breakfast. One by one, they take up their places; by ten o'clock at the latest they're all comfortable in their seats and ready to go. A row of seven wicker chairs, their legs somewhat sunk in the sand, neatly next to each other as if waiting for Snow White. And seated on the chairs, the seven of them, confidences and gossip flying over their heads from one end of the row to the other, hairdos still preserved despite their just-once-a-month hairdresser visit, all of them laughing and talking at the same time, cocking their heads this way and that, as if watching a game of tennis where, instead of one, a multitude of balls flies all over the place. Faster than anything else are their hands: cooing feathery birds, bulging and jumping about frantically as if in furious erotic dance, punctuated by the shiny knitting needles that emerge like antennae through the finger knot. However absorbing the discussion, their hands never slow down. Each one works on her own narrow little patch, yet they are all part of the vast knitwork that stretches across the row of chairs. At every third knot, they throw a loop left or right, holding the seven pieces together, with no gap or difference in knitting style. They start from scratch every morning, from a plastic bowl full of skeins at their feet and needles meticulously polished, good as new. The first line is always in brown tones: from sun-faded beige to roasted halva brown, depending on their mood. Slowly the lines darken, the beige becoming more chocolate, and the halva almost burnt from too much roasting. After half an hour or so, as

if agreed, with none of them leading or giving a signal,
but all of them riding the crest of a common breath so
large that the front legs of the chairs detach from the sand
and lean backwards, all seven yawning bodies spread out
in seven seas and break out in a frothy whiteness like
a mad dog's drivel, gently but irreversibly stabbing the
brown. Their hands work faster now. The needles often
strike each other furiously, frothing in the white momen-
tum. And then, once again all of them together without
even a nod, they start throwing in the blue. A little here, a
little there, ocean stains emerge from the froth like knitting errors, hiccups of excitement forever imprinted in
wool. Around noon, white is completely replaced by blue,
or sometimes by a deep sea-green and even gold if any
of them remembered to bring the golden skein. They always finish in the same way: a thin line, blue and cloudless
running all along the knit. The moment they cut the last
thread with their teeth, they let the needles drop from their
hands. They lean gently backwards in a slow oceanic arch,
and as the backs of their chairs sink deeper in the sand,
the seven of them pull the sea to their chins and sleep a
soft sleep until the following day. ◉

Embrace

They woke up earlier than usual. This time, it was not because of the little one crying. They just woke up. They opened their eyes at the same time and looked at the ceiling, while the baby–just seven months old–was still asleep. They took her gently in their arms and walked down to the shore. All they had with them was a dolphin-shaped inflatable toy dinghy: the baby girl's water cradle. They placed it on the surface of the sea, with the little one nestled in it, happily asleep. They entered the sea slowly, taking care not to wound the water, soft as placenta, dense as history, theirs as homecoming, virgin as it would be until the beach crowds came and spoiled it. They began walking slowly in the water, the inflatable dinghy between them: eyes half-closed, lung-gills and hand-fins, their breaths in sync with the breath of the morning water, with no after and no because. Slowly, the inflatable began to grow and stretch, sprouting masts and a stern, a toy sailboat that caught the wind in its sails and went forth. The slightest breeze sufficed. The dinghy carried on, bloated and swaying, reluctant at first with its portholes still facing its parents, and then more determined, swallowing mouthfuls of sea and climbing up breaths that only it could see. Its parents watched it sail away, enfolded in a map spanning the whole of the sea, traces of absence smooth and pointed, with the sailboat at the top and the world at its base. They did not stop walking, as their footsteps gradually began to sprout water roots, seaweed tentacles that made them slow down, build houses and households and futures

with every step. Around them, in sweeping circles, ships
were gathering like mountain crests surrounding a valley.
Soaring and magnificent, they cast their shadow on the
sea and gently closed around them. They had returned to
the womb. ◉

Constellations

I

It almost had no identity, no character, it was hard to re-
call it. It was never at the forefront of her mind, only as an
afterthought, a scent that had been there all along but had
by now become part of her skin, so much herself that she
no longer recognised it. She often lived in that moment
just beyond the mountains, pushed its silky green folds
lightly with her body and softened up a niche for her skin
to bathe in at the end of her tiring days. She would spread
out the seconds of that moment like a Japanese fan, each
little fraction of time another gilded fold, languidly sep-
arated from the one before and the one after. She often
moved that fan in her repose, her hands just underneath
the water surface, their contours already indiscernible
in the thickness of the green, her gestures impeded and
abandoned, always in need of a bit more air, a kinder
breeze, a forest breath. In vain, of course. Whatever wind
there was, it was always trapped in that moment beyond
the mountains, static even when at its most ferocious, nothing moving yet everything losing its place. She stooped
up the mountains every morning, her large heavy sack
thrown across her back. She had no time to lose, no Sundays or days of rest, no weeks of sacred holiness or evil in-
dolence, no dallying daybreaks and late dawns. She knew
that the task was vast and humbling–like her determina-
tion to carry on. Her life was only a tiny part of the task's
life, a dodged sacrifice to infinity that got her out of bed

ry. The landscape changed daily, the rainwater swelling down the slopes and turning previously reliable footing unsafe; or the billowing dust entering her mouth and breath, leaving her gasping like a new-born that had just been emptied out of the amniotic fluid's smoothness. High-er up towards the mountain tops, the snow would cushion her conscience and lull her into restful nightmares, but she knew what lay behind that steel blue warmth, and she carried on. Every so often, she would let her sack wobble off her back and roll onto the ground–a moment of relief from its shifting weight. She would briefly rummage in-side, knowing what she was looking for but almost never finding it right away. When she eventually did, she'd cup it in the palm of her hand and place it on the ground. Nev-er any hesitation–as if a line connected what she held in her hand with the spot on the ground where it was des-tined to go. Linking the dots. But the dots were runny and wobbly, the lines wet and fuzzy, origin and destina-tion bleeding into each other like hastily applied water-colours. The scoops were not even enough to create little puddles. They were immediately absorbed by the ground, whether cracking from parching heat or contracting from brittle snow cold. As soon as the water left her hand and touched the surface, even during that infinitesimal slid-ing of the first drop of the scoop, round and tense in its hesitation, holding back its force, wanting to rise up back into the hand but finally ceding to the gravity below, even during that moment, the ground was opening up, mouth and arms of a planetary beast swallowing up what little was being returned to it: no gratitude, no relief, just due return. It took her the whole day to spread the water from her sack onto the spots on her path. Some days the ascent was easier, less treacherous, more obviously entrapping. It was more honest in its threat than the descent, which often folded horizons of free falls and rumbling slides behind every apparently firm stone. Other days, it was the ascent that exhausted her, a climb up the oiled knees of an elusive god, asking her to prove her faith again and again with every scratch and wound. She never looked back at her work, but it tailed her like a string of saliva from the mouth of a dog; it followed her like the tattered end of a nuptial gown celebrating her marriage to the earth. Even at the driest of her days, when her lips were cracking with the one single continuous fissure reaching all the way to the thirsty earth beneath her, even at those times when she was most immersed in the rocky angularity of her task, she knew, or perhaps not knew but felt, or not even felt but just quietly quivered along a knowledge: that her true lover was elsewhere.

II

She was four or five years old when it happened. One of those white round days on the beach, with the sun under her eyelids and the sand under her fingernails, she was doing what she loved most: sticking long and thin pieces of wood in the mud as deep as she could. She collected the wood every day–at least thirty pieces, sometimes more, depending on whether there had been a storm the previous night and the sea had washed them out–as many as she could cram into her small plastic bucket, the one with the image of a train going round and round, and off she went. The spot had to be right: neither too soft nor too hard; not many waves, nor completely stale water, just a shallow pool at the edge of the sea, protected from too much movement and commotion. It also had to be away from the umbrellas and the cabins, ideally somewhere where the bathers wouldn't go, except for the very restless ones that walked all the way to the end of the beach as if they were trying to mark the place with their explorer's flag. This was tricky, because she had to be quick while her parents were not watching. She had often been told off for straying too far, "stay where we can see you" they kept on saying, "wear your hat", "don't distract yourself, there is lunch soon". She never meant to stray too far. It's just that her search for the perfect spot always pushed her further out, closer to the west end of the beach, where it is said–though she never herself saw it–that a shipwreck lies at the shallows, just off the coast. Her plan was simple: stick the pieces into the clay, as deep as possible but not so deep so that she could not see their ends peeking out, place them in close formation, one next to the other–her own private little forest buried deep in her secret spot.

Then rest a stone on them, the most beautiful stone she could find, large and flat and freckled, gold specks catching the midday sun, grey crevasses holding shade, rough and smooth interchanging, pretty when dry, prettier when licked by the water, a surface that could retain the round splashes like jewels on a pale wrist. And, finally, sit back and watch. It would not take long. Even when the ripples were becoming afterthoughts and the water drowsed under the blistering sun, even when there was no wind to cool her skin and open the day to the tiniest of breaths, the stone lasted only a short time. The sticks would scatter, the sand would retreat, and the stone would sink, a void full of weight collapsing under its own gravitas, a forgotten Ariadne inviting the sands and the waves to cover her up and close over her humiliated desire for permanence and radiance. On such a day, the older girl came up to her. She might have been followed by her through the day, but she did not realise a thing, so involved was she with her collecting and setting up. The girl loomed above her just when the stone started sinking in the sand. Unsmiling, she even kicked a bit of sand on top of the stone to make it disappear faster, and said, why are you doing this stupid thing, everyone knows that the stone is heavier than the wood pieces. She stood there, crouched and fragile, not knowing what to answer. It never occurred to her that the stone was not going to sink. It never occurred to her to think otherwise. The older girl went on, you do the same thing every day, I've seen you, what are you, some kind

of idiot, the girl's harsh voice sounding more and more
irritated, becoming louder and more resonant in the soft
recesses of her young mind, destined to become a rever-
beration that would never leave her.

III

The higher up the mountain she was climbing, the more
stentorian the voice. The lower she was sliding, the deeper
its resonance. After all these years, the voice had become
part of her, a mother that screamed even more than her
own, now long-dead. She even evoked it herself sometimes, a manic summons to discipline–show me my futili-
ty, tell me when I should stop, save me–but, no, not really,
she mistrusted that superego howling in her ears with the
wind, words by now all vowels, a train of limits and prohi-
bitions. Yet she allowed the guilt and fear to nestle in her,
day in day out, up and down the mountain, never stopping,
never allowing herself to become dissuaded by the voice,
remaining always in a constant, vain conflict. Only at that
moment–what was it–just beyond the mountains, where
she ended up after her descent–what was it–soft under the
shadow of the mountain, unperturbed by a single undu-
lation, the surface of the water restful, protected from the
raging waves of the voice. That moment, where the waters
finally emerge and the voice finally recedes. That moment,
where her body spreads like a starfish stretching over infinity. She reached the moment nearly always sweaty, ex-

hausted, satisfied with her day's work, undaunted by the looming cathedral of a task casting its shadow across her future and beyond her death, with a castrated elation that had no obvious object but its very own reflection. And she would glide in the glistening surface, soft green blankets sucking her in, seaweed wrapped around her limbs and tying her to the world, gold-speckled mud raising her to spires that caught the setting sun, fossilised sticks of wood, now gigantic and rising, gently thrusting her up deep in the orange sky. This was her island city, a receptacle of her body and her desires, splendidly isolated, tentacularly connected. The surface, heavy with water and waiting, would sometimes gradually boil up to cover her, and other times swiftly drain, leaving her skin moist with the memory of the flow. At times like this, when her body was closer to the sky, she turned to look at the mountain she had just descended. The slope was shimmering with the memory of her aquatic weaving, knot after knot of water deposits on this tapestry shrugged over the earth. Of course, nothing could be seen any more. She alone could trace the spots and trail the lines she had walked on, the constellations of a liquid night sky whose names no one will remember when the moment ends. But she was already looking at it from the other side, a diffused moment beyond life and death floating on the darkening evening. She often withdrew into that moment. She could forgive herself here. It didn't matter that her task was infinitely unfulfilled. It did not matter a bit, regardless of what the voice might have been saying out there. It did not even matter that here there was no special role for her, no place dedicated to her. Here, everything was calm, everything was swimming in a voluptuous connection to everything else. Everything was part of a wave that makes and un- makes cities, words and worlds. Here, time was no longer her enemy but a body to lie along and listen to. Here, time was as fragile as she was, barely keeping itself together, yet persevering with its slow crawl towards the end of the horizon. She always kept the last scoop for that city. She didn't rummage for it in her sack, offering it to the wa- ter like she did when she was on the ground. Rather, she took the sack with her when plunging in and, at the right moment, opened it slightly and let the city flood in. And the city, with its palaces and boats, pets and honeysuckles, pigeons and screaming seagulls, tourists and shopkeep- ers, its unborn and its forgotten people, would all stream into the sack, along with the city's past and future, its wa- ter underbelly and its celestial cupola, its endless repeti- tions across the planet, all this would crowd into the sack, search for the last scoop of water, gently unite itself with it and stay still for yet another day. ◉

and our island, in the middle of the lake, in the tender centre of an angular world, on whose shores one evening we hung to dry the texts for the planet's unconscious, will call us eternally to return. Can you hear the whisper of the night dresses, all taffeta and fear and water? Or even those rose bites that grew gills, so soft that became mother? Our work, this slow toil of poetic undoing, never ends.

Andreas Philippopoulos-Mihalopoulos is an academic /
artist / fiction author. His practice includes legal theory /
performance / ecological pedagogy / lawscaping /
performance lecture / video art / spatial justice /
moving-poems / critical autopoiesis / digital performance /
radical ontologies / installation art / picpoetry /
performance machines / fiction writing / sculpture /
wavewriting / political geography / clay making / gender
and queer studies / painting / continental philosophy /
posthumanism / anthropocenes. His work can be found at
andreaspm.com